This Puddinhead Book Belongs to:

The Puddinhead Story

_____

_____

_____

_____

The Puddinhead Story

Written by
Mary Ann DiBattista & Sandra J. Finn

Illustrations by Patrick Bresnahan

BookMasters, Inc.
30 Amberwood Parkway
Ashland, Ohio 44805
www.bookmasters.com
1-800-537-6727

First published August, 2008.

ISBN: 978-0-615-24552-2

Library of Congress Control Number: 2008907221

Printed in the United States of America by
BookMasters, Inc. 30 Amberwood Parkway
Ashland, Ohio 44805
Printed: August, 2009
Job#: M6441

This book is printed on acid-free paper.

To our husbands, Nick and Bill,
for all of their love and support.

To our children,
for the wonderful Puddinhead memories.

To our children's spouses,
for embracing our family traditions.

To our grandchildren—
May they enjoy and cherish family traditions.

Santa has a lot of work
to do on Christmas Eve,

Getting to each child's house
with presents he must leave.

He asked an elf named Puddinhead
      if he could help him out.

"Oh goodness, Santa, sure I will,"
      the little elf did shout.

He wondered what one little elf
      could do on Christmas Eve

To help get Santa to each house
      with presents he must leave.

"I want to make sure all the children
                    are asleep, you see,

So I have time to put these presents
                    underneath their tree.

If I stopped to talk to
      every child on Christmas Eve

I would not have the time to leave
      the presents I must leave."

The little elf, he thought and thought
about his given task.

Then he went to Santa with the
questions he would ask.

"How will I get from door to door
            and do it lightning fast?

How will I know just where to go?
            Who's first and who is last?"

Santa smiled, laughed, and said,
           "That's easy, my dear elf.

I'll give you special Christmas powers
           like I have myself.

You'll have the speed
        to get around,
            a list of where to go,

And you'll find each house
            that's on your list,
                even in the snow.

So tell me, Puddinhead, my friend,
         your plan for Christmas Eve,

To help me get to every house
         with presents I must leave."

"I think I know just what to do,"
the little elf did say.

"I'll put pajamas at their door;
they'll know you're on your way."

The word spread swiftly
    'round the world
        about this little elf,

Who quickly drops off
    every single package
        by himself.

Now when you get pajamas
    at your door on Christmas Eve,

It means that Santa's on his way
    with presents he must leave.

So hurry, put your pj's on
    and jump right into bed,

And drift right off to sleep with
    thoughts of Christmas in your head.

Many children sit and wait
        to catch this little elf.

Others say he's just too fast,
        but you can try yourself.

Author Mary Ann DiBattista lives in Westerville, Ohio, with her husband, Nick. They stay busy with three children and seven grandchildren. She is a graduate of Youngstown State University.

Author Sandra Finn lives in Valparaiso, Indiana with her husband, Bill. They have four children and six grandchildren. She also attended Youngstown State University.

The authors are sisters, born and raised in Youngstown, Ohio. Their father, Sam Zappi, still resides in Youngstown and has been a great source of encouragement. Experiences with their growing families were a motivating factor in the writing of this book. Their hope is that this tradition will continue for generations to come.

Patrick Bresnahan is a Design Engineer/Graphic Designer who is making his debut here as a children's book Illustrator. Pat lives in Columbus, Ohio with his wife, Kelly, and two children. He graduated from Bradford and is the son of author Mary Ann.

Dino Carlos is the Web Developer and Designer for the book and authors website. He lives in Indianapolis, Indiana with his wife, Michelle, and son. Dino graduated from Indiana University and is the son-in-law of author Sandra.

Not only is this story a family tradition, it is truly a family project.

We'd love to hear from you

Send us your comments,
drawings, or stories about
your experience with our tradition.

Write to:
Puddinhead
P.O. Box 2971
Westerville, Ohio 43086-2971

or contact us at:
www.thepuddinheadstory.com

My Favorite Puddinhead Memories